BELINDA BROWN

David McKee

Andersen Press

Belinda Brown just loved bananas,
she ate them for breakfast while still in pyjamas.

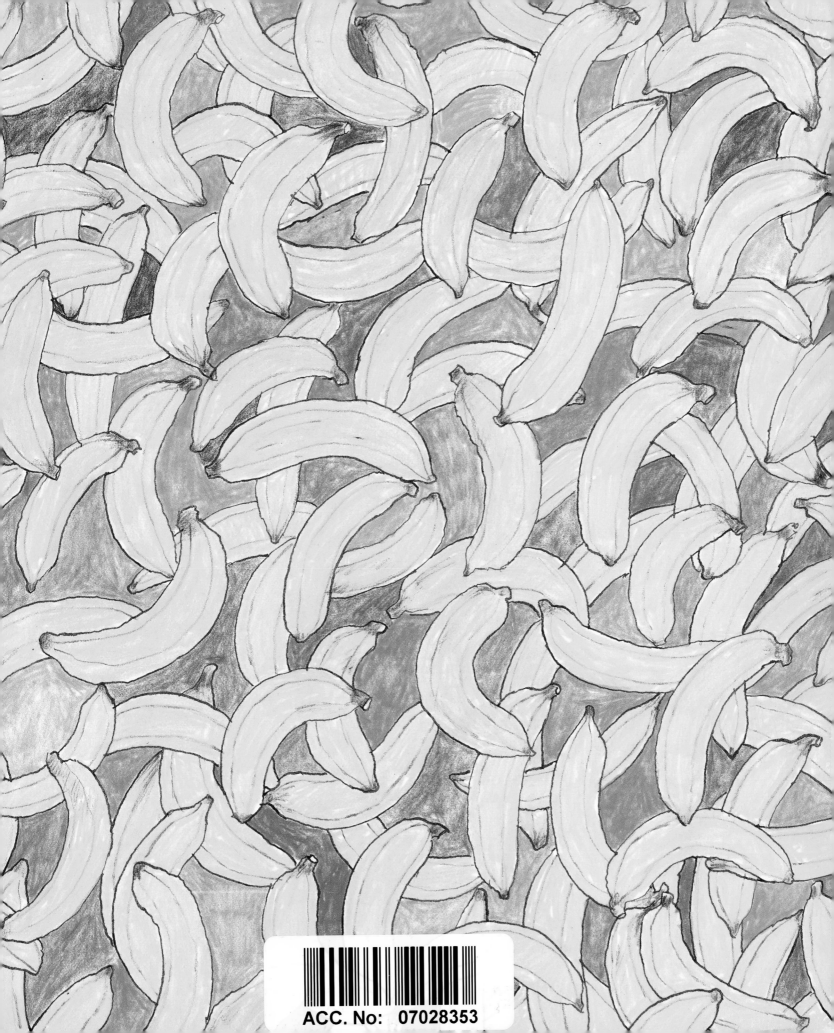

First published in Great Britain in 2018 by Andersen Press Ltd.,
20 Vauxhall Bridge Road, London SW1V 2SA.
Copyright © David McKee, 2018.
The right of David McKee to be identified as
the author and illustrator of this work has been
asserted by him in accordance with the
Copyright, Designs and Patents Act, 1988.
All rights reserved.
Printed in Malaysia.
First edition.
British Library Cataloguing in Publication Data available.
ISBN 978 1 78344 617 9

She peeled another at ten by the clock
and (in case she was peckish) kept one in her sock.

Brother Bryan gobbled burgers, biscuits and bakes,
bangers, buns, brioche and for breakfast? Bran flakes.

Aunt Sally, Belinda's father's mother's daughter,
ate hardly a thing and mostly drank water.

For lunch there was meat and two veg on the plate
but it was only bananas that Belinda Brown ate.

Cousin Norris was sporty and ate with great care:
healthy fruit, leafy greens... or whatever was there.

And what did BB chant when the time came for tea?
Why, "Bananas, bananas, bananas for me!"

Felicity Jones was Belinda's best friend
until a banana brought that to an end.

In the evening the family Brown all ate together.
They talked of politics, art and the weather.

The meal would be long, from start to dessert.
Miss Bee ate bananas till you'd think she would hurt!

The twins ate bananas as well, it is true.
Not a lot, in fact only the one between two.

Should Belinda feel hungry during the night,
she'd munch a banana without any light.

Mr Brown didn't care – he was busy and wealthy.
Besides, he'd read somewhere that bananas were healthy.

So Belinda peeled another and blissfully smiled.
"Healthy, so healthy," repeated the child.

Mrs Brown in her turn thought bananas not bad.
"Anyway," she would say, "it's only a fad."

Grandma ate chocolates, read and just sat,
but she knew what went on thanks to Spy, the cat.

Well, Belinda continued to eat yellow fruit
and no one around her gave even a hoot.

No one, that is, except Grandma Brown.
She worried, and worry is hard to keep down.

She beckoned Belinda to go for a walk.
Bee understood: Grandma wanted to talk.

"Too many bananas," Gran said, "and you'll pay the price:
a banana-shaped body that no one thinks nice!"

Belinda didn't want a banana-shaped back
but imagine no bananas except for a snack!

She decided to counter the symptoms instead
by walking around with a weight on her head.

She wore her hair high to cover the weight.
"That," she said, "should keep my lovely back straight."

Bananas won't bend your back, that I confess.
But a weight on the head? The rest you can guess.